THE GIGGLES ARE COMING!

CHRISTOPHER ELIOPOULOS

DIAL BOOKS FOR YOUNG READERS

For Jeremy & Justin

DIAL BOOKS FOR YOUNG READERS
An imprint of Penguin Random House LLC, New York

First published in the United States of America by Dial Books for Young Readers,
an imprint of Penguin Random House LLC, 2021

Visit us at penguinrandomhouse.com.

Library of Congress Cataloging-in-Publication Data is available.
ISBN 9780593109311 • Manufactured in China • 10 9 8 7 6 5 4 3 2 1

Designed by Jason Henry • Text set in Avenir
The artwork for this book was created digitally.

We were going to have **so much fun this year!**

It was our first day of school!

My best friend, Noodles, and I were going to be in the same class.

We put our backpacks in our cubbies.

Tried out the art supplies.

And met a new friend.

I LIKE YOUR HAT!

I LIKE YOURS!

I'M RUBY!

Then it happened.

Our new teacher, Miss Terri, started telling us about herself—

and I said it.

It was too late. They had us surrounded!

We covered our eyes.

We covered our ears.

But it was no use.

The **GIGGLES** tickled us.

We couldn't resist them.

I started to **GIGGLE!**

Then Noodles would **GIGGLE!**

And Ruby would **GIGGLE!**

Then I would

some more.

Then Noodles would

some more.

And Ruby would

some more.

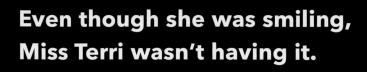

Even though she was smiling,
Miss Terri wasn't having it.

LET'S ALL SETTLE DOWN, PLEASE.

Then out of nowhere...

I tried to keep Noodles from laughing.
We were going to get in trouble.

But it was too late.

When we looked up at Miss Terri...

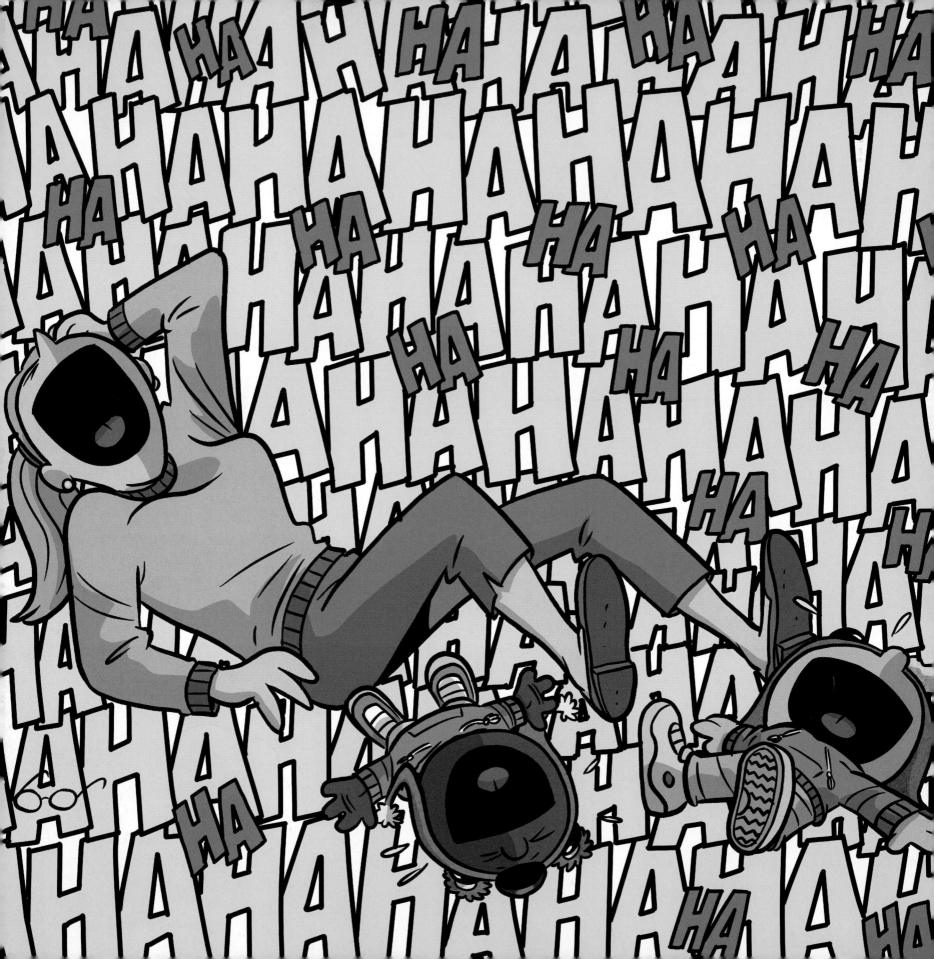

We were going to have **so much fun this year!**